CLIMBERS

Things That Move – Climbers
Things That Move – Flyers
Things That Move – Jumpers
Things That Move – Swimmers

Front cover *Koala, New South Wales, Australia.*
Back cover *Mountaineer climbing a frozen waterfall.*

First published in 1991 by
Firefly Books Limited
61 Western Road, Hove
East Sussex BN3 1JD, England

© Copyright 1991 Firefly Books Limited

© Copyright Jillian Powell (text)

The moral right of the author has been asserted

Editors: Francesca Motisi and Caroline Maw
Designers: Jean and Robert Wheeler

British Library Cataloguing in Publication Data
Powell, Jillian
  Climbers
  1. Motion
  I. Title   II. Series
  531.11

  HARDBACK ISBN 1–85485–101–2

  PAPERBACK ISBN 1–85485–169–1

Typeset by DP Press Limited, Sevenoaks, Kent
Printed and bound by Casterman, S.A., Belgium

CLIMBERS

Written by Jillian Powell

Monkeys and apes are good climbers.
They have long arms and legs for
swinging through the trees and strong
fingers and toes for gripping branches.

4

The mountain goat climbs up steep mountains to find grass and plants to eat. It has special hoofs to help it grip on to rock and ice.

Cats climb
easily. Their
sharp claws
help them grip
and their long
tails help them
balance.

Squirrels live in trees, building their nests high up in the branches. They climb up and down to find nuts, seeds, fruits and berries.

When a baby koala is born, it
rides on its mother's back. Soon
it will learn to climb, using its
long fingers and toes, and sharp
claws to grip.

8

Tree frogs
have long
legs and
special feet
which help
them climb.
Under their
toes are
sticky pads
which hold
on to leaves
and bark.

9

The gecko is a small lizard which lives in hot countries. It can climb easily because it has scales like tiny hooks under its toes.

Chameleons are a kind of lizard
which can change colour to hide
from their enemies. As they
climb they use their toes to grip.

Sloths climb very slowly through the
trees, moving one arm or leg at a time.
Their long claws hook round branches
as they hang upside-down.

Tree snakes have special scales
on their skin which help them
grip on to bark as they climb.

Spiders climb easily with their eight legs. They spin lines of silk to make their webs and sometimes swing from one place to another.

In dry, sunny weather snails
sometimes climb plant stems to
escape from the heat of the ground.

Caterpillars have many pairs of
legs for climbing. Some have tiny
hooks around their legs which
help them grip.

Firefighters climb tall buildings to put out fires and rescue people in danger. They use long ladders or special fire-engine cranes with platforms.

Steeplejacks climb
tall buildings to
repair them. They
use special ladders
which clip on to
the chimney
or building.

18

Cable cars carry
people up
mountains. They
climb high
over the trees
and houses.

Mountaineers climb
mountains for sport.
When they are climbing on
heavy snow and ice, they need
warm clothes and special boots.

Rock climbers climb with their hands
and feet, using ropes and spikes.

These children are having fun
climbing! If you live in the town or
the country you can always find
somewhere to climb. Make sure you
are with a grown-up.

Notes for adults

This book teaches children that they are not the only ones than can climb all over the place! Stunning photography shows the many different types of animal that can climb – from koala bears to the more familiar domestic cat. People are also shown climbing – sometimes for a living e.g. firefighters and steeplejacks, and sometimes for pleasure e.g. mountaineers and rock climbers. Here are some discussion points and questions relating to the pictures.

Discussion points

Page no.

5 Ask the child if s/he can remember why mountain goats have to climb steep mountains.

6 Ask the child whether s/he has seen a cat climb a tree. Ask the child why s/he thinks cats climb trees (e.g. if they are frightened, to chase a bird or to sharpen their claws).

8 These are koala bears which live only in the gum trees of Australia. Explain that although they look like a small bear, they are marsupials (with a pouch which holds the young while they are growing).

11 Ask the child if s/he can remember why chameleons change colour.

13 Ask the child why s/he thinks snakes climb trees (to hunt for lizards or birds).

17 Ask the child if s/he can remember why firefighters climb tall buildings.

18 Ask the child if s/he can remember the word for people who climb buildings to repair them.

20/21 Ask the child the difference between a mountaineer and a rock climber. Talk about the special equipment needed for these sports.

Picture Acknowledgements
The photographs in this book were supplied by: Bruce Coleman Ltd. 10 (Hans Reinhard), 20 (Keith Gunnar); Oxford Scientific Films *front cover* (P. Harris), 4 (Mickey Gibson), 5 (David Fritts), 7 (Anna Walsh), 11 (Zigleszczyynski), 13 (Michael Fogden), 14 (Harold Taylor), 15 (Robert Maier), 16 (© Mantis Wildlife Films); Mountain Camera 21; Topham Picture Library 19; Timothy Woodcock 22, 23; Zefa *back cover*, 6, 8, 9, 12, 17, 18 (both).